JE GLE

Glease, Hannah E.
Magic tree and the flyaway
birds WITHDRAWN

D1306982

The
MAGIC TREE
and the
FLYAWAY BIRDS

Published by Ray Rourke Publishing Company, Inc.,
Windermere, Florida 32786.
Copyright © 1980 Piper Books Ltd.
Copyright © 1981 Ray Rourke Publishing Company, Inc.
All rights reserved. No part of this book may
be reproduced or utilized in any form or by any
means, electronic or mechanical including
photocopying, recording or by any information
storage and retrieval system, without permission
in writing from the publisher.

Library of Congress Cataloging in Publication Data

Glease, Hannah E.
  The magic tree and the flyaway birds.

  SUMMARY: The animals living in and near the magic oak
tree witness the seasonal activities of a redstart
family, including its winter migration. Includes
suggested activities such as finding the animals con-
cealed in several drawings.
  [1. Forest animals—Fiction.   2. Birds—Fiction]
I. Embleton, Gillian.   II. Title.
PZ7.G481446Mad   [E]   81-102
ISBN 0-86592-102-4   AACR2

The MAGIC TREE and the FLYAWAY BIRDS

By Hannah E. Glease

Illustrated by Gillian Embleton

Ray Rourke Publishing Company, Inc.
Windermere, Florida 32786

Atchison Library
Atchison, Kansas

811169

In deepest woodland stood an oak
That often smiled but never spoke

Upon its trunk so old and lined
It had a face for *you* to find

For no grown-up can ever see
The features of a magic tree

The animals and birds all knew
Exactly where this wise tree grew

They gathered in the leafy glade
And took protection from its shade

Two squirrels in its mouth had found
A safe dry home, well off the ground

And just above, beneath its brow
An owl perched on a bending bough

Some badgers burrowed underground
In tunnels spreading far around

And butterflies and birds and bees
Flew in from all the other trees

This story tells of one sad day
When a pair of redstarts flew away

Atchison Library
Atchison, Kansas

In a crooked branch, just by the magic tree's "brow", there was a nest. In it lived two redstarts and their chicks. All day long the parent birds brought food for the chicks: beakfuls of caterpillars, worms and flies.

Back and forth the redstarts flew. The magic tree and the animals that lived in its care watched the chirping nestlings grow. Soon they were so fat and feathery there was no room to turn in the nest.

It was time for the young ones to leave home. "You must learn to fly," said their mother as she pushed the chicks from the nest. "Oh, don't let them fall," the rabbits cried. "They'll hurt themselves," the

badgers sighed. But no harm came to the little birds. "Goodbye," they chirped, as they flew away. "Maybe you'll come and see us one day. If you can find us in our new homes." Can *you* see the birds in the leaves?

The redstarts were too sad even to sing when their chicks had gone. Soon summer had gone, too. Green leaves had turned to gold. The animals made their winter beds and got ready to sleep.

14

All but the redstarts. The birds were nowhere to be found, and their nest lay in bits on the ground. "Oh, what can have happened?" said the hedgehog. "I fear for their lives," croaked the frog. The magic tree said nothing.

Far and wide the animals searched. But, as they feared, there was no trace of the birds. The redstarts had truly disappeared. As the winter snowstorms fell, the animals stopped looking. It was their turn to disappear.

To hide them from the prowling fox, the tree magically turned their fur all white and sent them to sleep in a warm blanket of snow. Can *you* see where the animals are hidden?

One day in spring the animals heard a sound they all knew well. It was the song of the redstarts. "Where have you been?" they cried and crowded around to hear. Together the redstarts told their tale.

"We've been to lands across the sea, where the sun shines all the time. The animals are twice as large as any that you've seen. There are lions with manes, and zebras with stripes, and giraffes as tall as trees."

The animals all shook their heads and whispered to the tree: "We don't believe a word they've said. We're sure it can't be true." But the magic tree only smiled to itself, for it knew the birds' tale was true.

The same thing happened every year when the redstarts came back home. They built their nest, and laid their eggs and taught their chicks to fly. Then off they went to seek the sun and never said "Goodbye."

This story told of one sad day, when a pair of redstarts flew away.

Play and Learn

1 Talking helps children learn. Discuss the story with them. Talk about the tree, the birds and the other animals in the story.

2 Get them to show you the tree's face, its eyes and nose. See if they can point to the owl, the badgers and the rabbits.

3 Ask them about the colors of things in the pictures.

4 Ask how many chicks there are in the nest, how many birds are hidden in the leaves (pages 10 & 11), how many zebra, how many giraffes, and so on.

5 Can they name all the animals in the pictures that are not mentioned in the text? Can they find and name the animals hidden in the snow?

6 Talk about the big African animals at the end of the book. Tell them why birds migrate — for warmer weather and food.

7 Tell them how birds lay eggs and sit on them to keep them warm.

8 Encourage them to take an interest in birds and put out food for them, especially when it is cold. Tell them the names of the birds they see in the garden or street (sparrows, pigeons, blackbirds).

9 See if you can find an oak tree; or a tree with a 'face' on it. Collect some oak leaves and some acorns.

10 Ask them to tell you a story about birds or paint a picture of the magic tree.

Atchison Library
Atchison, Kansas